The Happiness Flower

By Eva-Lis Wuorio

The Happiness Flower

by
EVA-LIS WUORIO

Illustrated by
DON BOLOGNESE

The World Publishing Company
Cleveland and New York

Published by The World Publishing Company
2231 West 110th Street, Cleveland, Ohio 44102
Published simultaneously in Canada by
Nelson, Foster & Scott Ltd.
Library of Congress catalog card number: 68-26973
Text Copyright © 1969 by Eva-Lis Wuorio
Illustrations Copyright © 1969 by The World Publishing Company
Designed by Jack Jaget

For my mother

JUNE 24, 1968

Prologue

THE SUN poured through the schoolroom windows. The snow had at long last gone.

The wooden, yellow-stained desks felt like a prison.

They had seemed safe and comfortable in the long winter days. Then the sun came out only to say hello, and by the time you'd said hello back, it had gone on to the other side of the world. One would ski home in the dusk. Lights would gleam welcoming from the windows. There would be the smell of dinner cooking. Lessons would be done by firelight.

The days were short in winter. They began with darkness in the morning. They ended in darkness before one even intended to go to bed.

But now it was entirely different. Light had come back. The sun was still up when grownups claimed it was time for children to go to sleep. Light washed the

7

walls and roofs of rooms and squeezed in through drowsy eyelids long before breakfast time. The thawing earth sent up scents of spring and growth. Every day new flowers appeared in the gardens, in woods, and in fields and by the hedges. Melting ice left a slurruping, lovely, sloshing song in the ditches, swelled rivulets into rushing streams, sang of light and warmth and coming summer.

In the marshes golden buttercups lifted bright faces out of their shiny green leaves. In the woods the blue hepaticas mingled with the white, spotting the moss with the colors of Finland. Blue and white. Blue for the skies and lakes and bordering seas of the dear land. White for the long snows, the white clouds that speckled the summer skies, the white flowers that sent, spendthrift, their scent into the welcoming bright evenings.

The children stirred uneasily in their prison of learning. Their feet itched to be out of shoes. Any minute now it would be warm enough to swim, to put the boats into water, to open up the cabin on the lake in the woods, to get going with a million splendid summer things.

Winter was finished. Summer was here. School just hung on too long. Three months of freedom were only a few days away.

Old Miss Söderström had a hard time keeping her face straight and strict as she lectured the class on this, one of the last afternoons of the school year.

She was thin and tall and kindly and she loved them all.

She had been a teacher in this small village all her life. She had seen it grow until it was nearly a town. The fathers and the mothers, even a few grandfathers and grandmothers, of the children squiggling in the seats before her, quivering with eagerness to rush into summer, had sat in this same classroom. She could recognize the family likenesses so well that sometimes, accidentally, she called the children by the names of their parents.

She made her voice as stern as she could manage. She said:

"Now you will not forget, not a single one of you, will you? You'll have to collect your flowers. You've taken down the instructions? Pekka! If you blow another spitball at Jaakko you'll stay after school. How many flowers will you bring me back the first day of school in September?"

Pekka jumped to his feet. His grin was as wide as his face. "Twenty-five, all perfect specimens. I'm to throw away the ones I ruin when I'm pressing and pasting them."

"And," Miss Söderström continued, "I am *not*, I repeat, *not*, having you turning up with your mother's or father's or cousin's collections. I remember well when Pekka's father proudly presented me with a very neatly pressed and well-labeled book of flowers. He forgot that I'd marked them myself when I first saw them eight years before, when his eldest sister collected them. The paper had even yellowed. He hadn't thought of that!"

"My uncle is almost as young as me," Lena stood

9

up and said, laughing. Discipline relaxed during the last days of the term. "And he used his brother's collection once, and you found out. But then he went to another school and has a collection you haven't seen, Miss Söderström, and he said I could use that this year if I didn't get mine done in time!"

The class roared with laughter.

"You are dreadful, just dreadful, all of you." Miss Söderström flung her arms about in despair, trying to keep from laughing too. "I remember how Maia's Uncle Matti came with her Aunt Ulla's collection one year. But I'm not having it, you hear. Maia, are you with us?

The thin girl with the thick shock of straight blond hair turned reluctantly from the window. Someone had said "Maia," hadn't she? She'd just seen a swallow in the birch tree outside. A little winged messenger from far Africa, come to tell cold old northern Finland that summer had come.

"Yes, I will, Miss Söderström," she said absently.

Everyone laughed again. Maia blushed.

The old teacher said quickly, "We were talking about the flowers. You won't forget now, will you, Maia? Remember, children, pick carefully. Don't waste any. Flowers don't like to be picked and thrown away. Choose your specimens and bring them home in your box. And then what?"

"Clean the roots, but not with water," Jaakko said. "Water will make them mold. Press them. Change the blotting paper every day, if necessary. Fix the gum. Label them correctly. May we go now?"

"You won't be any happier to see the last of me than I will be to see the last of you," Miss Söderström said sharply. "Yes, you may go now."

Unobtrusively she moved toward Maia's desk. She didn't want to ask her to stay behind in front of the rest of the children but she rather expected her to loiter behind the others. Maia had always been a shy child, but in the past six months she'd had the kindly old teacher really worried.

Miss Söderström stopped at the window, waiting for Maia to collect her things and look up, watching the children hurl themselves into the sunlight. Half of them would do their summer chore of collecting flowers right away, she knew. Half of them would leave it until the last few days of the vacation. She could always tell. Some came back with spring, early summer, mid-summer, late summer, autumn flowers. Others had just a hastily done muddle of the flowers of fall. Well. Children were children.

All the same it made her happy to think that all through the long, lake-speckled, forest-green summer land there would be children taking time to notice a flower. Perhaps, even if they didn't stop to pick it, they'd see the beauty of it.

She couldn't remember who'd started the whole thing, perhaps Linnaeus, the founder of the modern systematic botany, himself, two hundred years ago. But it was a good thing, she thought. It was a pleasant duty. And it would surely open the dullest child's eyes to the miracle of growth and the constant blessed beauty of the world.

"Maia," she said, as the slim, long-legged girl finally stood up from her desk. "I did want to have a word with you, child."

"I know I've not done very well this year." The girl looked her straight into the eyes. "I'm sorry."

"Well, we figured out one problem. You do need glasses. Lots of people get absent-minded and inattentive when it bothers them to look at things. Gives you headaches."

"Oh, Miss Söderström, I do so hate the thought of them!"

"I know. Your mother agreed that you should have the summer to practice on them before wearing them to school. But your grades have fallen very, very badly." Miss Söderström knew the main reason for Maia's failure. Her parents had decided to separate some six months ago. Maia adored her father and after he went away she had suddenly become a changed child, but she was by no means stupid.

"Am I going to fail my year, Miss Söderström? Is that what you want to tell me?"

Normally, Maia certainly would have failed her year. But Miss Söderström made her judgments by her long teaching experience, with her heart and prayer to God, not by school-board requirements.

She said, "I was thinking, Maia, that if your flower collection showed application and thought, you could go on to the next grade in the fall. I want to see you apply yourself to work again. I want proof of it. And you are not just to go off by yourself, you know."

"I see, Miss Söderström," Maia said. "Thank you."

Miss Söderström turned to tidy her desk. If only the child would bring a nice collection of flowers, she'd feel justified in having passed her when her grades really didn't warrant passing.

Such a lonely, such a puzzled child. It would be unfair to fail her this year. But, Miss Söderström told herself sharply, Maia would have to pull up her marks in the new school year.

Chapter One

THE FIRST morning of the summer holidays Maia's mother let her sleep as long as she wished. That was the first treat of summer. All the same, she came down to the neat blue-and-white kitchen well before eight in the morning.

Maia's mother was scrambling eggs because that was Maia's favorite breakfast. She smiled at her. Maia's short hair was golden as a ripe rye field in the sun, her marimekko frock was as blue as her eyes, but her bare feet were still so winter-white they looked cold.

"I'm afraid it's going to be a bit lonely for you this vacation, small daughter," Mother said. "As you know I've been offered a summer job to take the place of people who go on their holidays, and you know, the money will be useful."

"That's all right," Maia said. "I'll just be lazy, and there'll be lots of time to read."

"You remember our agreement?"

"Yes," Maia said with a sigh. She pulled the dreadful case out of the pocket of her marimekko. She took out the glasses and pushed them slowly up her nose. "I can't see my scrambled eggs any better."

"You know the doctor said the glasses were mainly for reading and writing." Her mother couldn't help smiling at Maia's woeful face.

"They press down on my nose bone too."

"The agreement was that you could get used to them during the summer, before wearing them to school."

"I look such an awful moron in them."

"You don't look anything of the sort," her mother said, though privately she thought Maia looked a bit like a lovable frog, as Maia had chosen large round-rimmed glasses. "You look sweet and you are mine."

"Oh, well," Maia said. "I won't need to wear them for doing dishes. I'll do those, and dust, and sweep the porch and the path."

"And then why don't you take a couple of sandwiches down to the lake? I heard old Kalle say he's painted the rowboat. It's probably dry by now, and in water."

Maia's thoughts flew as she got down to the household tasks. Summer was so many things. She made a song and a tune out of her head as she worked. *Green, green grass, smelling so sweet as I pass, tickling my nose as I roll on the grass, green new grass. Summer rain, washing the trees, washing the bees, then sun again. Rainbows over the lake and sky, as on the rocks by the shore I lie.*

Pretty soon everything was done. She didn't mind keeping the little house tidy. She'd been helping her mother as long as she remembered. Her father had too, before he went away. But she wasn't going to think of that. However hard her parents had tried to explain their separation to her, she didn't want to understand it, or even think about it.

The glasses were enough to worry about. She didn't like them either—not one little bit. She'd promised to practice wearing them, so she would, but it was just one more thing.

There were daisies in the field at the bottom of the garden and buttercups in the ditches. She loitered down and picked a bunch big enough to fill the large yellow earthen jug. When she was very little her father used to reach down for her hand and say, "Let's go and pick some flowers for Mummy." And always when they came back her mother's eyes would shine and she'd clap her hands and say, "How lovely! Thank you, my Maia."

And now it was nearly lunchtime, and suddenly the day seemed to lengthen out, long and empty and lonely.

Of course it was lucky her mother had found summer work, Maia told herself, but it would have been nicer if she'd been free.

Slowly she began to make herself a sandwich. One would do. She didn't feel a bit hungry.

She wouldn't go down to the shore either. She didn't feel like talking even to old Kalle.

Perhaps she'd walk up to the pine woods. There was a southern slope there where the wild strawberries might be ripe.

But she wouldn't take a book. Then she wouldn't have to use the glasses.

But she'd take them with her. A promise was a promise.

Her feet lagged.

The sun still shone, the breeze rippled over the fields, the larks sang.

But somehow laughter had gone out of the day.

Chapter Two

BY THE END of the first week of holidays Maia just couldn't figure out what to do to fill out the rest of the eleven free weeks.

Her mother had begun to send anxious glances at her too.

Their little house was on the edge of the village. On the farms closest to them the children were either much older than Maia, or babies. Her best friend had moved away to a distant city just about the same time her father had gone away.

"Hadn't you better start your flower collection pretty soon?" Mother asked that morning as she was setting off on her bicycle.

"There's plenty of time," Maia said. "Weeks and weeks."

"That's what everyone always thinks. Then, suddenly, puff, the summer's over," Mother said. "At least, do get your press out, and make a list of the new things you'll need. I'm sure we'll have to buy a few extra bits and pieces."

Maia went down to open the gate by the well. She waved to her mother until she disappeared around the curve of the lane, and that was when Maia suddenly decided it was a day for an adventure.

It didn't look like the right sort of a day at all. Clouds were racing across the sky and the wind was crispening, but Maia had been feeling so contrary without knowing why at all, that this day seemed to her just right.

She got out her jeans and sturdy sandals. She'd go to the Blue Mountains, or at least as close as she could get. She'd take her flower-collecting case with her. That would be a good excuse for making the trip. But she doubted very much if she could be bothered picking any. She just didn't feel like it.

She made a cheese sandwich and a herring sandwich, and packed them and two tomatoes and an orange into the collecting case. That at least made it useful.

The ridge of the hills on the horizon had a way of never seeming to be the same shape or the same distance away. In different lights, at different times of the year, the hills drew closer, or receded farther. They had a businesslike name on all the maps, but Maia had called them the Blue Mountains as long as she could remember talking or even just thinking about them. There was always a shimmering blue light on the peaks and the sky seemed especially blue above them.

Every summer of her life her family had rowed across the lake in picnic parties to pick blueberries in the level woods, or in the autumn to spend the whole day filling baskets of whortleberries on the heath. There was also a marsh where the lake ran out into a stream, where the golden brambleberry grew.

This time she was going to go much, much farther. Perhaps she could get all the way to the top of the nearest mountain.

She hadn't thought of taking the rowboat. But as she came down the fields to where the shore path skirted the fields and the lake, she saw it. Kalle had painted it pale blue with white gunwales again this summer. It was tied up at the end of the little wooden dock.

It was a nice small boat. Her father had had it specially built for her mother so that it would be light and easy to handle. In other summers her mother would often say just before bedtime, "Let's go for a spot of evening fishing."

This year they hadn't gone out once, yet. Her mother just looked tired at the end of the day.

Maia knew that the oars would be in the dressing room of the sauna, on the shore. The wind whispered in the shore willows and the waves slapped against the rocks as she carried the oars down. For a moment she thought she might just paddle around to the little water-lily bay. Then she felt stubborn. No. She'd go all the way to the Blue Mountains.

On the path she nearly stepped on the three-

pronged *vanamo*. It was so fragile, the bell-like flowers purple-pink, that she stopped and considered picking it. She even remembered its proper name because it was for the father of botanists, Linnaeus, and for the northern lights: *Linnaea borealis.*

I'll pick it on the way back. I've nowhere to put it now anyhow, she thought. The box is full of my lunch.

The wind was stronger than it had felt on land. And it was against her. While it was not a very big lake at this end, it was big enough for anyone of Maia's age and size. There were islands, of course, so every so often she could get into the lee of them and have a rest. But it was well past noon when she got across to the other side.

The sky had darkened by then. A thin shower of rain slapped at her face. The shore line was forbidding. There really seemed no place to land at all.

She could barely make out the tiny sauna building at Kotiranta (that means "home shore," which was the name of their inlet) across the lake. And she was feeling guilty. She knew that, while she was allowed to take the boat out *inside the rushes* at Kotiranta, she wouldn't have got permission to cross the lake by herself had she asked for it, which she hadn't.

But she was still feeling contrary. She *was* going to the Blue Mountains. If she could find a place to shore the boat . . .

There was no place to land. Trees and brush came to the water's edge. Her collecting case was slapping against her arm and chest. The rain was coming harder. Some of the wet on her own face was salty.

Finally she saw a gap between two rocks. There was a little pebbly beach beyond them. She could tie the boat to a sturdy juniper bush leaning out from the shore.

She rowed into the gap. Because of the two boulders she hadn't any room for her oars. She'd have to pull the boat in.

She got out and the water was way above her knees. Cold and wavy.

Sobbing a little she got hold of the painter and clambered up the shore, trying to pull the boat after her.

A hairy hand reached out of the juniper bush.

It grabbed the painter, gave a yank, and the rowboat crunched up onto the pebbly beach, secure.

A gruff grumbling voice said, "What's the matter with you, girl? You've only gotten a little wet. *I've* got a *thorn* in my *toe!*"

Chapter Three

MAIA didn't have time to be scared.

She was so surprised.

The little man who hobbled out of the juniper bush was no taller than she was. He was wearing a moss-colored leather jerkin. His leather pants ended at his ankles. His feet were somewhat large and a little hairy.

"*Entäs sitten! Entäs sitten!* What do you want!" the little man said in his gruff irritated voice. "Stop staring. No manners. Stop blubbering. What summer rain wets, summer sun dries. Not long the rain. I'll stop the wind. First things first. What are you going to do about my thorn?"

"I was just surprised," Maia said. "Thank you for pulling my boat up."

"Helpless, that's what you looked. Shouldn't go out alone if you can't look after yourself. Blubbering. It's a warm enough day. Won't do people any harm to get the summer rain on their shoulders. Makes them grow, Peaked, that's what you are. Skin and bones. Too short."

"I'm not that old yet," Maia said indignantly. She was about to add that he wasn't very tall himself when she saw him lurch on his foot; he bit his lip, and one green tear fell from his green eye.

"Let me have a look at your toe," she said. "Sit here."

On the higher boulder they were sheltered by the pines from the drizzle. The rain really seemed to be stopping. There were blue patches between the clouds.

The peculiar little man seemed suddenly so worried that Maia didn't mind at all lifting his hairy foot on her knee.

"Sorry my jeans are wet," she said. As she lifted the foot it blurred in front of her eyes. Then she remembered. The glasses.

She got them out of her pocket. The little man watched intently as she took them out of the case and slid them up her nose. Now she saw that the feet were really very clean for anyone walking barefoot, and the hairs were fine and golden.

She asked, "Does it hurt at the bottom?"

"At the side. Between the big toe and the next toe."

"Oh," Maia said, "why, it's a thorn as big as a spike. No wonder it hurts! Shut your eyes and hold tight."

27

She got her fingers firmly on the thorn and yanked fast. That was the way Mother always took out splinters when she could get hold of them and didn't have to use a needle.

"My goodness," she said. "You *are* brave. Look how big it is!"

"Yes I am. So I am. Indeed I am. I'm brave indeed," the little man said. He didn't sound so gruff now. "I've walked ever so far and ever so wide and ever so bright and ever so light with that *perkele* in my toe. Why, I think it's infected. Could you put some earth-good on it, please, young friend?"

"Earth-good?" Maia said, puzzled.

"Women of old," the little man said impatiently, "always made good healing things from plants of the earth. You are only a little woman but surely you have the gift."

"Well," said Maia, sort of pleased with what he had hoped she could do, "I haven't anything with me. But perhaps, just perhaps, the orange would do."

Her mother put iodine, or some sort of salve, on her scratches and wounds. They always made everything sting worse for a minute. The orange wasn't very sweet at all. Perhaps it would have a sting.

"You just wait," she said, and got her flower-collecting case. While he watched her sharply, she opened it and got out an orange.

"Oh," she said. "But I've not brought my *puukko!* I can't cut it."

"Oh yes, you can," the little man said. She didn't see where he had found it but suddenly in his hand

29

there was a *puukko* of shining steel. (*Puukko* is a little dagger that even children in Finland are allowed to carry; of course they are told how dangerous it is to use it in a fight, and how useful it is for cutting fruit, or digging up flowers with their roots, or peeling potatoes.)

Maia immediately cut the orange in half.

"Now," she said, "while you suck this half, I'll squeeze the other half into your wound. It has vitamins. It ought to fix everything."

"This is the funniest looking apple I've ever seen," the peculiar little man said, "or is it a foreign type of potato? It doesn't grow in any of my trees and I've never seen it in any of my earth, and I've gone far and I've gone wide and the things I know are long and they are high—and the fruit I've eaten is found by the lakes and on the tundra, in the woods and on the lowlands, by the rushing great rivers and under stones."

"Oh, do stop it," Maia said. "Just eat it. It's good for you. Every time we can afford it we have it. In some countries they even eat it for breakfast *every day.*"

"What's it good for, then?"

"For dessert. And for strength. I told you it was full of vitamins and that's good for you. Now you rest for a minute and I'll give you half of my lunch, or," she said a little regretfully, "as much of it as you'd like."

They sat under the pines, sheltered by the juniper bushes, very companionably.

Below them, across the lake, gusts of rain fell into half rainbows. At times Maia could see the sauna at Kotiranta so clearly it seemed no distance at all. At times it was entirely hidden in a shower.

She said, munching a quarter of her cheese sandwich (the little man had taken all the rest without so much as a thank you), "I was going to go to the top of the Blue Mountains today."

"It's a long way and a good way and a way that may not always lead there, but the end is not the big thing. The way itself is the best," the little man said.

"I don't understand you at all."

"You will when you put your mind to it at a high moon and a high noon and the time when your heart is ripe for it and your thoughts fly like eagles."

"I like the sound of what you say," Maia said, "but I really don't quite know what you mean."

"That's the meaning of words," the little old man said. "Words are there for trying to plumb for the hidden meaning of things, and words are there to hide the meaning, and people searching for the truth will put words to their own imaginings and still not reach the end of the meaning. Aha. You don't get that either. But let it rest. One night you'll wake and there will be moonshine across the foot of your bed and you'll remember what I've said."

"Do you mean to tell me we'll never meet again?" Maia dropped the rest of her small bit of sandwich.

"Pick that up; it's very rare but quite tasty. Only pine needles stuck to it. Pine needles never hurt anyone. Very healthy. Yes, of course we'll meet if you wish, and I wish, and you need me and there's aid I can give. What's the matter with you anyhow?"

Maia thought for a long moment. There were a number of things on the edge of her mind and all of them seemed to matter. She picked on the simplest.

"I have to get twenty-five flowers this summer," she said. "I'll have to press them and take them back to school with me in the fall."

"What's the matter with you then, child?" the little old man asked. "Look under your foot. See the tiny little star I can't see with my own old eyes. But I feel it's there."

"I can't see it either," Maia said.

"What about the magic eyes you carry in your pocket?" the little old man asked accusingly. "I saw you put on a magic eye to look at the thorn in my toe. You look at that flower now, and then perhaps you'll let me have a peep through them too?"

Chapter Four

MAIA flew home in the little boat as though it had a sail blown full by a kind wind.

Her mother ran out of the sauna to the little porch above the lake and shouted, "Darling child! *Kulta lapsi!* Where have you been? I've been so worried."

"Only picking flowers," Maia said, "and exploring, and seeing the friends of the woods."

Somehow she felt a little reluctant about talking, even to her mother, about the little old man.

She knew he existed, but at the same time, since she'd left him, he seemed like a *peikko* from a storybook. She knew in the Finnish woods there lived little people, gnomes and elves, *tonttuja* and *peikkoja*, trolls and goblins and kindly dwarfs. There were also the great ancient pagan heroes of Kalevala who sometimes

33

on summer evenings came to sing their songs in the lands they had to leave when Christianity came to Finland. No one doubted that the magic people of the older ages existed.

But it was very difficult, suddenly, to say that she'd met one of them.

"I'm sorry I am late. I'm sorry I went so far," she said. "It was only across the lake and I can row well."

Her mother was so happy to see her that all she said was, "I've got your flower press out. Old Kalle is bringing new bricks for weights. And I bought sheets of blotting paper, all in pretty colors this year."

Maia remembered the *vanamo* then, the flower she had almost stepped on in the morning. But they were already halfway up the path. She could always get it in the morning.

In the little study which had hardly been used since her father went away, her mother had put out the two big, heavy old boards. She had dusted them and already brought in a couple of bricks for weight. There was also a stack of wide pastel-colored blotting paper ready to use.

Suddenly Maia realized how worried her mother must have been to start preparing a surprise for her, rather than making tea or putting clothes to soak, or other ordinary chores. And she hadn't been scolded. She'd hardly been scolded at all since Father went away. Her mother just looked sad, which made it very difficult to be naughty even when one felt like it.

It was a good thing there was a present from her too. It was a tiny flower that *looked* like a *vanamo*, but not quite. It shone like a star when you turned it to the light. It was called "Heart's Desire," the little man of the woods had said.

"Don't press it, child," he'd warned her. "Put it into good black earth in a little brown pot; give it seventeen drops of spring water each morning and each evening. I'll show you a spring in the woods which has just the right water for this little plant; you can take some home in a bottle. It should be watered at sunset. But never mind, people who are lucky enough not to have a sunset at all shouldn't complain. Better light than darkness, I always say. Watch it glow. It's a Happiness Flower."

Maia couldn't think of a better present to give to her mother. So first of all they planted it, taking care to see that the spray of spindly roots had room to go straight down.

Maia said, "I've got a plan for collecting things this year." (Actually it was the idea of the little old man of the forest.) "I'm going to do it in families. Of course I'm going to pick up other things I see as well, like bluebells and daisies and the blue hepatica and the *vanamo*, but what I'm really going to do is a series of flower families."

Her mother watched her glowing face and though her heart tugged just a little at the word "family," because their family was broken, she felt content to see Maia happy again.

She said, "Let's see what you have got, *kultani*." (*Kultani* in Finnish means "my golden one," just about the same thing as "dearest.")

35

"Well, you see, Mummy, the buttercup is not just a yellow buttercup in the meadow. Buttercups have relatives in the mountains and the ditches and marshes, and by the river, and even in Lapland. The one that grows in the ditches by the road is called *Ranunculus*

ficaria, and the one by the river, *jokileinikki,* is called in Latin *Ranunculus lingua,* and there is the one that grows on the hills called *Ranunculus bulbosus,* and those are the only three I've got today. Look how different their leaves are, the green leaves, and how fat the yellow petals of the flower are in some, and how fine in the others."

She grinned, a little embarrassed. "I saw the difference better with my glasses, Mummy."

She took out from her collecting box the three yellow plants from the others she had picked.

"Do you see, Mummy, do you see the difference, and the sameness of them as well? I'll still have to get the *Ranunculus flammula, repens, acer, auricomus, sceleratus, glacialis,* and *peltatus.* That's all of that family that grows in our Finland, ten of them."

"*Kultani!* How you spout out those Latin names! I never knew you had taken such interest in flowers!"

"Oh well, you see, someone told me that one used Latin names so everyone could understand—like Esperanto that old Miss Söderström was so keen on. If one calls flowers by their family name in Latin, everyone all over the world will know just what you mean. After all, if I say *Kevätleinikki,* how is anyone else except a Finn to know that's a *leinikki* that comes out in the spring?"

Maia started cleaning the roots carefully, shaking them free of earth and dusting them with soft paper tissues. It would have been easier to wash them, but then mold could set in. She had to cut the roots and the bulbs of the *Ranunculus ficaria* carefully, with her

37

puukko. Otherwise they'd have been too thick to press. Then she put each plant, carefully, between two sheets of blotting paper. It was a difficult, slow job. You had to open the petals of the flower and the leaves on the stems very carefully to get a good pressing.

"The prettiest of that buttercup family," the old man of the forest had said after he'd borrowed Maia's glasses and studied the three plants they'd picked, "is the *Ranunculus glacialis*. I'll see if I can find one for you. Will you let me look at things with your magic eyes again?"

He'd thrown himself on his stomach and had a chat with an ant.

"Tomorrow?" Maia had asked.

"Sure, and why not, tomorrow." Reluctantly, he handed the glasses back to Maia. "Why, I haven't see old Busy-busy so clearly since I was a boy, quite a few hundreds of years ago."

Remembering this, Maia asked, "Mummy, could I take a bottle of iodine with me tomorrow? One does get thorns into one's toes."

"Yes, do," her mother said because she knew Maia was a responsible child.

All the same she thought it was curious.

Chapter Five

FOR A MOMENT she thought that the little old man wasn't going to be there after all.

She rowed to the landing place between the two boulders. The way across on this bright golden morning seemed much shorter than the day before.

The only things that had seemed long were the dusting and sweeping she had done before she left home.

Then the hairy hand suddenly came out of the juniper bush, seized the painter of the rowboat from her grasp, and the growly voice grunted, "The hole where the thorn came out of my toe hurts."

"I've brought just the right stuff to put on it." Maia slipped into the water and didn't mind getting wet. "It'll sting, mind."

Because the sun was high and hot and bright, and the sky arched clear pale blue, she was wearing shorts. Legs always dried. It was clothes that took such a long time.

"So you remembered." The little old man chuckled. "You're a nice child. Right out of the roots of the trees and the sands of the seas and the flickering sunlight, the evening star bright. What's your name?"

"Maia."

"Maia," he said. "Grumph-garooh. Not bad. Just

right. But you ought not to give your name out so readily."

"Why not, old man of the woods?"

"Words are important. There's magic in words. In names, most particularly."

"What's your name then, old man of the wood?"

"Oho! Oho!" he said. "You've given me a good name. Tells nothing and tells everything, the name you gave me does. If you want to call me anything else at all, why, just call me Peikko."

"But that only means a troll, a sort of kindly goblin," Maia said. "It's not a name, not a proper one. It's like calling me Girl, or Human. Are you a troll?"

"Let's say I am and let's say I'm not. I've a proper name of course but to give away such a private secret is always a mistake. So, if you want to call me Peikko, I'm willing if you are. I've been about so long that I know what I'm saying and if the end's well the beginning's well too."

"You use an awful lot of words for secrecy."

"I use them as I see fit," Peikko answered shortly. "Are you going to let me use your magic eyes if I help you find flowers?"

"Of course I am," Maia said. "I hadn't thought of them as magic eyes at all."

She handed them to Peikko and immediately the little man lay down on his stomach and began to watch the ants, saying, "I must see what the Busy-busies are up to today. And oh, and by the way to boot, look for my little green sack there by the stone."

Maia had to search for some time.

Peikko's little green sack was the color of moss and the color of juniper bush sewn up with threads the color of lichen. Maia finally found it only because a friendly ladybird landed on it. When she picked it up it weighed nothing, but by the time she had brought it to the little old man, flat on his stomach, talking to the ants, it seemed to weigh a ton.

"I tell you, this old Matti Busy-busy is the most interesting ant I've known in centuries." The little old man looked rather foolish with Maia's glasses. He would have looked more foolish if she hadn't gotten such big rims for them.

"I've always made friends with ants," he continued, "mainly from the point of view of curiosity. They work so hard. Busy, busy, busy, all the time. I just can't understand it because I'd rather do nothing, unless necessary. But a conversation with them does no harm. It's as good as an education."

"Here's your little green sack, Peikko," Maia said.

"Ah, so there it is. So you found it. Shows that you are one of the right ones, the good ones, the real ones. Some might not have noticed the differences in the colors of green. You should take up painting. Well, well then. Open it. I brought you a present."

There were seven rather limp flowers. One was pinkish and one white and the rest yellow. They didn't look like much.

"*Sillä siisti*, that's good then," the little old man cried. "There's one of the family missing, but you have to do something yourself. Aren't you even going to thank me?"

"Thank you very much, Peikko, and thank you also for the buttercup family. I've brought you an orange for lunch and some cheese sandwiches as well."

"There's another little thing I'd like to ask you," Peikko said. He looked slightly embarrassed. It occurred to Maia he wasn't used to asking for favors from anybody.

"I don't think I can get you any glasses if that's what you mean," Maia said. "Unless you want to come to the doctor with me, because he looks at your eyes before he gives you the right sort."

"I wasn't thinking of a *grand* favor like that," Peikko said. "I was just hoping you'd let me use them for a purpose of my own."

"Is it too secret to tell me?"

"Well and now and this and that," Peikko said. "I might not tell everyone, or anybody for that matter. But I've made up my mind to tell it to you."

"What is it, then?"

"I want to see three wild ducks in a row eating blackberries," Peikko said and muttered to himself, "I've tried from the bushes and I've tried from the hills, and I've peered through the blades of corn and peeked through a field of rye."

"I don't see how three wild ducks in a row could ever get at blackberries," Maia said.

"All right, then I don't see how I can get you whole families of flowers when some of them grow in the spring and others grow in the autumn and some of them grow in the south and some of them come up only once a year in a Lapland tundra."

43

"I didn't say I didn't *want* to help you," Maia said. "I just said I didn't know how I could."

"You could look for them with your magic eyes."

Peikko kicked angrily at a piece of moss. There was a stone inside it. He'd hit his sore toe on it. "Ouch," he said and a green tear fell from his green eye.

"Dear Peikko," Maia said, "these glasses only see *very near*. That's why I'm not supposed to read without glasses."

"How can you see *very far* then?"

"With my own eyes," Maia said. "Look, I can see a duck and some ducklings by the bushes near our own sauna shore. And I can see an empty bird's nest on the top of the pine tree. It's only little close-by things I can't see clearly."

"Use your eyes then, human child. Look for my three wild ducks eating blackberries, all in a row."

"May I ask, or is that a secret too, why it's important?"

"I might as well tell you. You are so curious about everything." Peikko bit heartily into a cheese sandwich and Maia was glad she'd made lots of them today. "It's because I'm bored."

"Bored?"

"Oh, you know, tired of hanging about the same old place all the time. That's why I let you see me, actually. I could just as easily have been invisible. Also, you were crying. And we peikkos—we don't like to see children crying."

"I know. Thank you," Maia said. "But what's going to happen when you do see those three wild ducks in a row, eating blackberries?"

44

"I'll be free to go to visit my various relatives. That's why I happened to think of you collecting *families* of flowers, because I was thinking of these various far-flung cousins of mine. There are the nisses in Norway, always drinking bowls of cream by the splendid fjords. And there are leprechauns in Ireland, that's on my grandmother's side of the family, who know a lot of good songs about treasures. Some of my German relatives have turned nasty, but the kobolds still hold perfectly good parties in the heights of the Black Forest. And in Brittany—but it's not necessary for you to know all this. Let's just say I've got relatives all the way there and all the way back, and at the sunrise and the sunset, and by the sea and under the sea, and in the Alps and above the Alps. I haven't seen any of them for some hundreds of years, and I'd just like to have a little bit of intellectual conversation."

"Why haven't you gone to see them then?"

"Busy, busy, busy," Peikko said. "You do ask too many questions. Shall we say, for example, that I did a bad turn once and that counts against us just as much as it counts against humans who turn nasty."

"So you are under a spell?"

"You could put it like that. What are you going to do about it?"

"I'll help you of course," Maia said. "I'll keep an eye open for those three wild ducks eating blackberries. And you won't have to think you are under an obligation. I'm going to do it because I love you."

"Oh, you've been reading the dictionary again," Peikko said. "Obligation's bobligation gobligation fobligation between friends. Of course I'll help you get your

45

flowers. Which family are we going to collect next? Is there another sandwich? Oh, you *are* a good human girl. You've brought me that delicious golden apple."

And without even peeling it, or offering to share it with Maia, he bit into the orange she'd brought for lunch for both of them.

He looked very happy.

Chapter Six

THAT NIGHT, when Maia had gone to bed, her mother tidied up around the house.

The bricks on top of Maia's flower press had slipped sideways and as she adjusted them some of the blotting paper slipped out, too.

She picked it up to put it back between the press, thinking to herself that Maia had been much happier since she started on her flower collecting.

The flower was a pinkish white with curious fern-like leaves. Maia had made a note beside it saying it was *Ranunculus glacialis*.

Her mother looked at it a long time and thought how very curious it was she'd never seen a buttercup like that. She'd always been fond of flowers and had lots of books to tell her how to grow them and where they would grow best.

She found the right book of flowers on one of the book shelves that lined the two walls of the little room her husband had used as a study.

And then she stared at the flower that Maia had pressed and at the picture of the flower in the book.

In the book it said that this very flower, the one Maia had so carefully pressed, "grew only in Lapland."

Where, she thought, could the child have found such a very rare specimen?

She looked at all the pictures of all the buttercup family, in the book. Then she looked at the ones Maia had picked. It was really extremely remarkable.

It's not very easy to find a family of flowers at any time, unless one is terribly keen on botany, and picks things all through the year. But here, in Maia's collection there were buttercups that grew in the spring, the summer, and the fall—by rivers and in the meadows and in the mountains.

Maia's mother put all the flowers back under the press very carefully, but she still was puzzled.

How could the child have gotten such a fabulous collection?

Sometimes, she thought, one just didn't do justice to children's industry and intelligence.

Chapter Seven

THE NEXT DAY it rained. And it rained the day
after. It rained for a whole week.

All the farmers were glad because it was good for
the fields. All the lumbermen were glad because it made
the rivers full of water so that logs, cut in winter,
rushed at great speed toward the sawmills. It was more
dangerous for the men in charge of the logs, but lumbermen liked danger. All the children were sad, except
the ones whose mothers let them splosh about in the
puddles and mud and rain.

Rainbows swept the sky and dropped the ends of
their arcs into fields of buttercups so that all the children, all over Finland, said, "Look, look, there is the
glow from the pot of gold at the end of the rainbow!"
(Except what they really said was, "*Katso, katso, tuolla*

se sateenkaaren kulta aarre kiiltää!" because, naturally, they spoke in Finnish.)

Apple blossoms fell and fruit began to grow. Strawberries came out like succulent red jewels on the green velvet of the wet leaves. Daisies and bluebells, clover and cornflowers made the fields look like gay patchwork quilts.

Maia picked them and pressed them and for a time forgot about her plan to collect whole families of flowers. It wasn't so easy anyhow, all by oneself.

Each day she planned to go and see Peikko, but after the rain came long golden days and time flew by. Every day she went to swim from the sauna shore and by the time she could bear to come out of the water it was too late to start rowing across the lake.

The wild duck family became so used to her, and so fond of the bread crumbs and tidbits she carried in her pockets for them, that they wouldn't even scatter when she swam.

They'd come to the sauna steps, the mother duck gliding regally, and the little ducklings straggling in a line behind her. There was always the one who got lost or couldn't keep up with the others.

Maia laughed at the way the mother duck would scold the stupid little one. And it was even funnier when they tried to dive, imitating their mother. They could never get their furry little bottoms under the water. They looked like the fluff of dandelions with a beak sticking out.

Then, one night, Maia awoke to the cracking thunder and stabbing lightning of a short summer thunderstorm.

She didn't know why, but immediately she thought of Peikko. He'd be safe and dry enough in his secret forest fastness, she consoled herself, but all the same she thought of him so hard she almost heard him call. She went back to sleep and dreamed of him, and when, very early, she awoke again, she was determined to go to see him that very morning.

She made an especially good and especially large picnic. Besides cheese and herring and potato pies, she put in wieners and cucumbers and what was left from the strawberry-cream cake from the night before.

Briskly she rowed across the lake with the wild duck and the ducklings squawking and clucking for their breakfast behind her. But when she came to the two big boulders the little beach looked terribly empty.

The pines rustled and soughed overhead. The morning still remembered the night's storm, with the wind blowing from erratic directions and a bit of rain slanting down from an unexpected cloud, unfinished rainbows patterning the sky. A squirrel, somewhere, chattered about lost pine cones. But below, the pine needles lay unstirred. There couldn't have been a fat furry foot stirring them up, there, for ages.

The peikko had seen his three wild ducks, eating blackberries, and gone off to visit his far relatives! She was suddenly sure of that. And very sad.

Why hadn't she come before! He was such a nice peikko.

She began to pull the boat up the shore. It was as difficult as ever.

She slipped on the rain-washed stones and fell.

That's when the hairy hand came out of the juniper and the gruff voice snapped, "Well, you've taken your time. And here's my sore toe festering, and I haven't had a golden apple for weeks!"

"Peikko! *Kulta* Peikko!" Maia picked herself up, not minding the scratches and bruises at all, only very happy that she'd remembered to bring him an orange.

Chapter Eight

THEY had a little snack right away. Peikko ate an orange because Maia said she was saving the strawberry-cream cake for later.

While he was eating, she looked at his toe. It was perfectly all right.

He had been fussing and complaining only because she had been away for so long. She grinned at him. Now she was sure he liked her.

He grinned back and licked his fingers clean. "I've got a new family of flowers for you," he said. "I expect they've all gone to ruin because you haven't been around to collect them."

"They'll be perfectly all right, with *you* looking after them," Maia said politely.

"As a matter of fact I did put them into damp

moss," Peikko said. "Funny thing, I got a lot of them while strolling in Lapland while it was raining down south here, and there was a very nice young man doing the same thing."

"What sort of a same thing?"

"Picking flowers," Peikko said. "He looked a little bit like you. Same hair, same eyes. Oh, all you humans look just a bit alike. We, the old people of the ancient times, we all look individual."

"*I* look individual," Maia said indignantly. "I look just like myself and no one else."

"That's what I like about you," Peikko said. "Spirit. Always shouting. But that's true of all you Finns. In a way I'm glad I'm a Finnish peikko. All the others know they can't step on my toes and that's for sure."

He went and fetched his little green sack.

"This is the Saxifraga family," he said. "Just look at them."

The flowers were little and wilted, but as he handled them they came back to life. They were very delicate and white and pale blue, pink, and yellow."

"I've seen some in the rocks, I think," Maia said.

"That's a fact." The old man of the forest nodded, pleased that she knew what she was talking about. "We'll go up to the top of the hill here. There you might find the one I didn't get for you. After all, you'll have to say where you found these things, won't you?"

"I can't accept another present from you, dear Peikko," Maia said. "I haven't seen three wild ducks in a row eating blackberries yet, and I doubt very much if I ever will."

"Never mind," Peikko said, "either you will or either you won't. There's a can and can't and may and may not to practically everything in the day and night and the dawn and twilight and the beginning and end. If you don't see them it's just my bad luck and I'll go on looking for another hundred years or so, but truth to tell, I *would* like to take a little trip, before youth passes me by. Well, let's go up the hill."

As they climbed the ever steepening path toward the peak of the blue range of hills, Peikko suggested they should chant the Finnish names of the Saxifraga family of flowers to keep their spirits up. They chanted:
"Tähtirikko,
    Pahtarikko,
        Sinirikko,
            Kultarikko,
                Nuokkorikko,
                    Lehtorikko,
                        Mäkirikko—
and Papelorikko!"

It made a perfectly good song.

The sloping hill meadow ended in pine woods. Still they climbed and they climbed. Purple heather grew under the towering red-trunked pines. Blueberries were ripe on their tall stems. They tasted cool and juicy and Maia began to think of blueberry pie.

"I know what you are thinking," Peikko said. "Yum, yum." He had an uncanny way of seeming to hear thoughts. "There was one of those pies on the window sill of a forest cabin once when I happened to be passing by. Yum, that smell! The pie happened to

57

fall just then and as I don't believe in waste, I happened to catch it. I can remember the taste still."

"It just *happened* to fall, did it, Peikko?" Maia laughed. "All right, we can pick my collecting box full of blueberries and the picnic basket as well, and I'll ask Mummy to make two pies and I'll bring you one."

"I'm a good picker in a good cause," Peikko said. "I picked a basketful of luscious mushrooms and put them on the window sill from where the pie fell. You should have seen her face!"

"Now I know how peikko stories start." Maia chuckled.

And they climbed on. Heather gave way to silvery gray moss, and red-granite boulders grew bigger and balder.

"Look, there," Peikko said. "*Saxifraga nivalis*. What you call *Pahtarikko*."

It was a little plant, about two inches high, with a furry stem and a cluster of small blue-white flowers. Maia got out her *puukko* and carefully dug it up, roots and all.

"Well and fine," Peikko said, "that completes *that* family."

A short stiff scramble up the cliff and finally they were on top.

Far below them lakes and rivers spread like blue lace between headlands, woods, and islands. There seemed to be more water than land, which, in this part of Finland, was just about true. Lacy, feathery clouds drifted in the wide arch of the sky.

It was so beautiful Maia felt breathless.

"I don't know how you can bear to leave Finland,

Peikko," she said. "Is there anywhere a lovelier land!"

"There's beauty everywhere on earth, different, that's true, but not less beautiful," Peikko said, seriously for him. "You'll find that's true when you get to my age and have traveled enough. Anyhow, I'll be coming back to the home woods after I've had a short chat and a bit of a natter and a meal or two and a fight and a dance, here and there and yonder. I've very interesting relatives, I have."

"But everywhere is so *far*," Maia said. "Look, even from here to home looks millions of miles away."

"But you made it, didn't you, and you've only legs. I've ways and I've means, and just as soon as I get the release, and the spell is broken, then go I must."

Maia sighed. "It does seem hopeless. I've never even seen three wild ducks in a row, much less three wild ducks in a row eating blackberries."

"No point in wasting time moaning and groaning," Peikko said. "How about that little snack out of your basket, so we'll have room for the blueberries?"

Peikko ate everything with such good appetite that Maia didn't even mind not getting her fair share. Then he asked to borrow her magic eyes, threw himself on his stomach, and told her he'd have a short Ant Visit.

"Different family of Busy-busies up here," he remarked. "I could certainly use a pair of your magic eyes in my business. There's a lot of minuscule—that means piddly and little—information going around I just can't seem to get at, not being able to see that well."

"I had never thought of my glasses in that way," Maia said. "I just thought, what a nuisance."

"That's because you don't use your brain. You

59

ought to take an interest in things. Let me tell you, a big blob of a thing is just dull unless you look into it and see all the little bits and pieces it's made up of."

"True enough," Maia said. "Flowers—the smaller they are, the more interesting they look through glasses."

"Don't stand there just chattering and nattering," Peikko grunted. "Get started on that blueberry pie!"

"I see what you mean." Maia grinned at him. "A big blob of a blueberry pie wouldn't be very interesting without the blueberries it's made up of, as you say, and *that*," she added sternly, "is bad grammar."

Slowly she worked her way down the hill, in the cool shade of the tall soughing pine trees, picking berries as she went. It was difficult to put them into the collecting case because it opened at the side, so she ate as many as she kept. She hadn't gotten it half full by the time Peikko joined her. He had the picnic basket brimming with lovely luscious dewy purple-blue berries.

"*Hyvänen aika!*" Maia said. "How could you do it so fast?"

"You haven't got the technique," Peikko said. He put out his hairy hand and swept it over the blueberry bushes and the berries seemed to jump as to a magnet. In a second Maia's case was brimming full.

So he immediately made a good, solid, old-fashioned birch-bark basket for her.

"Put your Saxifraga family in your collecting box," he said, "and I'll make us more blueberry baskets if need be."

It was getting on toward late afternoon when they

got back to the shore and Peikko came to help Maia push the rowboat into the water.

As she put the oars out, the wild duck mother glided toward the boat, and her ducklings, getting quite big and ugly now, no longer little yellow fluff balls, paddled after her.

"My goodness," Maia said. "I think it's my own duck from our *sauna ranta*. It must have followed me."

Peikko narrowed his eyes and stared at them, helter-skelter around their mother.

"Harrumff-harooof," he said. "Haven't seen a wild duck that close for a hundred years."

As Maia waved, and started to row, she thought she heard him mutter, "That human girl's a lucky one, lucky for her and lucky for me. That I knew. And what I knew, I know."

Chapter Nine

YES, of course Maia took a big delicious, succulent, delectable blueberry pie to Peikko the next day. He finished it in a flash, muttering to himself, "Ambrosial, nectareous, fit for a peikko. Pity there isn't more."

And the summer days passed, each seemingly long and lovely and lazy, but each month speeding by faster than a thought.

Maia and Peikko continued to collect flower families until Maia had a collection that was three times as big as it needed to be. By now she was so interested, however, in flower families that it didn't seem like a chore at all. It was fun.

Her mother, though she was puzzled about the occasional strange flowers Maia brought home, was content to see her Maia happy.

She didn't bring home only flowers for her collection but also strange and lovely flowers to plant or to put in vases, as well as berries and mushrooms, plants for the garden, and herbs for the kitchen.

Then, one evening, picking red currants and white currants and black currants from the bushes by the apple orchard fence, she suddenly felt chilly.

Twilight was near. Surely it wasn't that late!

It wasn't so late by clock hours, it was late by season. Summer had slipped away. Autumn was knocking at the evening gate.

She stared out across the fields to the twilit lake, the heights of the Blue Mountains held in the last light. She realized summer was past.

And with that problems came rushing back. There was the lonely ache for her father, so long gone, and no news from him this whole summer. Her glasses she didn't mind at all now. That was one problem that had disappeared. They did show her so many lovely, tiny things, as Peikko had said. But Peikko! He had helped her with her problem—but what about his?

She hadn't found him his three wild ducks sitting in a line, eating blackberries.

Absently she lifted the branch of black currants to her mouth. Her hand stopped half way. Black currants! Surely edible even for ducks! What berries could be blacker!

It might work.

She could at least try.

"Maia! *Kulta!* Maia!" her mother was calling. "Come in, come in. It's getting late and cool."

65

It always happened like that in life. Just when you decided to do something, the grownups had other ideas. Well, there was still a week to go until school started.

"Your collection is really remarkable," her mother said in a puzzled voice. "I've been looking at it through these magnifying glasses—we seem to have two of them, goodness knows why."

"Could I have one," Maia said quickly. "For my own, or even to give away?"

"Of course, *kultani*," her mother said and gave her a sandwich and a glass of warm milk.

Really, the child sometimes seemed to live in a world of her own. To whom could she possibly give the magnifying glass! She'd been alone the long summer through. But she hadn't seemed at all unhappy after the first week. Mother gave a little sigh. It was too bad adults so often broke up the world of a child.

Maia certainly wasn't unhappy.

As she went to sleep she thought that even if her first idea didn't work, at least she had a splendid present for Peikko.

She could hardly wait to see him look through his very own magnifying glass the first time!

Chapter Ten

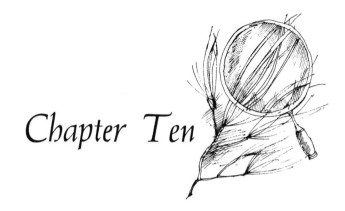

MAIA picked Peikko's birch-bark basket full of black currants the moment her mother had bicycled off to work the next morning.

Then she ran all the way to the *sauna ranta*.

There were birds winging in vast sweeps across the sky.

For a moment she had a horrible thought. The wild duck had left for the south! All the birds were beginning to go. She was too late with her wonderful idea!

Then she heard the cracked quacking from the rushes and the old duck glided to the sauna steps which led right into the water. Her brood cavorted behind her.

Maia threw out a small cluster of black currants.

The duck clucked at it, "That's not bread crumbs,

that's not what I'm used to!" It dove under the berries floating on the little ripples of waves, came up, and had another peck.

"Quack-glugg-cluck-cluck," it said and hoisted its tail in the air.

The duckling who had been the smallest and slowest to begin with had grown up to be the most rambunctious. It came roistering up now, flapping its wings, swimming and gliding and diving.

It seized the berries in its beak, tossed the little cluster in the air, caught it again, and clucked noisily, "Glugg-gglogg-gloood!"

Maia was sure she saw it smacking its beak, delighted with the taste. (I bet he wouldn't have liked real bitter old blackberries, Maia thought.) Its brothers and sisters rushed over to see what was up. They decided they liked black currants too. In fact they'd have liked anything, being greedy.

Maia ran down to the boat. The oars!

She ran back for the oars, and down the path to the little wooden wharf again.

"Come on, come on, duck family," she shouted. "Come with me, for a swim and berries."

As she rowed she kept scattering black-currant clusters after her. She'd rowed across the lake so often that by now the way seemed short. Or perhaps it was the rowing, and swimming, and good appetite, and summer sun that had made her stronger.

The duck family trailed behind her.

She was early, and she had not brought a picnic. She only thought of that as she edged the rowboat between the two sheltering boulders. Perhaps Peikko wouldn't be there!

There wasn't a furry hand coming out of the juniper bush to help her.

She could pull the boat up easily, herself, now. But usually he was there to give her a hand.

"Peikko! *Kulta* Peikko! *Tule, tuleppas!*" she called.

. Every so often she stopped calling to throw another handful of black currants into the water to keep the ducks happy. Even so, she thought, soon they would have eaten so much they wouldn't want any more.

She was getting really worried.

At last a growly gruff voice answered from the juniper bush.

"What's all the noise about, what's the noise about, then? I've been up all night, seeing to things—no reason to get up until it's eating time. Shouting and bellowing and screaming in the middle of a perfectly good dream. Did you bring anything to eat?"

"No," Maia said. "But I brought this."

She put the magnifying glass into his hand.

"Look at the hairs on your other hand. It's better than my magic eyes."

There was a long silence. Peikko stared at the hairs on his other hand. He picked up a pine needle and looked at it through the glass. He picked up an ant and studied it.

His voice was quite mellow and soft when he said, "Oh. Oh. Oh. It's the Veritable Glass Magnificent."

"And I'd forgotten," Maia shouted. "Look out on the lake!"

The mother duck and most of the nearly grown ducklings had gotten bored. They'd glided and spluttered off into the reeds to look for something tasty, or possibly to wait to escort Maia back, across the lake.

There were only three big ducklings left, lining up to try to get at the three remaining black-currant berries floating on the ripples of the waves before them.

"Three wild ducks in a row," Peikko whispered. "Eating black berries. Well, I never."

Chapter Eleven

MAIA hurried home. She wanted to make a picnic, even a late one, to take back across the lake to the very happy Peikko. The door of the house stood wide open. She stopped and stared.

She'd left it closed.

Then she saw the suitcases on the porch. There was a small car on the path by the well.

A tall, fair-haired man, who looked very much like her, only completely different, ran out of the house, down the steps, and swept her into his arms.

"Maia, my Maia," he said. "Goodness, I've missed you!"

Her mother came out too. There were tears in her eyes but they weren't sad tears.

Her father said, "If you two will have me back I'll never go away as long as I live."

73

Of course they said they'd have him back. After all, they'd missed him terribly.

So it was sort of natural that Maia forgot all about Peikko that day. It wasn't until they were having sandwiches and milk before going to bed that evening that she remembered.

It was because her father suddenly said:

"It's a funny thing. Like a blow on my head, suddenly one day I started thinking of Maia having to do her flower collection for school this year. So every time I had a moment I'd go up the fells and try to find her a plant or two. You'll think I'm silly, but it seemed to me I was always followed by a nattering little green man, a sort of peikko, who said I ought to get flowers of the same family. It was useless, he'd grunt right behind me, to go picking a flower here, and picking a flower there. Families were best."

He looked thoughtful and then he smiled. "So I began to think, too, that family is best."

He began to rummage in his luggage. (There had been lovely presents of Lapp boots and Lapp four-wind caps, and Lapp carvings for Maia and her mother.) He finally found between a pad of writing paper a very sad little collection of plants. All dried up.

"I had nothing there to fix them properly," he said sadly. "But I brought them anyhow."

"Never mind," Maia said. "I can make them as good as new."

"And you know what?" her father said. "That little *vanamo* type of flower you have in the pot on the kitchen window sill? I kept finding it everywhere. And

75

every time I saw it, somehow I thought of the two of you, and home, and the sauna path, and fishing in the evenings."

"Maia found it," her mother said. "She calls it the Happiness Flower."

"That's just what it is," the three of them said and smiled at one another.

To Finish Up:

I thought you'd like to know:

Kind old Miss Söderström and all the class were astonished about Maia's flower collection.

The other children immediately wanted to be friends with her and find out how she had done it.

Miss Söderström was rather puzzled about the variety and completeness of the flower families but when she heard Maia's father had come back from Lapland, she decided he must have helped her. And she was so glad to see Maia happy she wasn't going to fuss about *that*.

Maia did very well in school that year, and for many years after too. And it was not just because she wore her magic eyes, although of course that helped.

Sometimes she did stop to stare out of the schoolroom window on a spring morning and wonder whether Peikko had yet returned from his travels.

She never told anyone about him (until now) because as she grew older she realized she might not be believed.

But she never forgot him or the summer of the Happiness Flower.